For Lucy, who once told me about some BADDIES! – M. S.

For my own Naughty Naughty Baddies – D. T. x

Bloomsbury Publishing, London, Oxford, New York, New Delhi and Sydney
First published in Great Britain in 2017 by Bloomsbury Publishing Plc
50 Bedford Square, London WC1B 3DP

www.bloomsbury.com

BLOOMSBURY is a registered trademark of Bloomsbury Publishing Plc

Text copyright © Mark Sperring 2017
Illustrations copyright © David Tazzyman 2017

The moral rights of the author and illustrator have been asserted

A CIP catalogue record for this book is available from the British Library

ISBN 978 1 4088 4972 9 (HB)
ISBN 978 1 4088 4973 6 (PB)
ISBN 978 1 4088 4971 2 (eBook)

All papers used by Bloomsbury Publishing are natural, recyclable products made from wood grown in
well managed forests. The manufacturing processes conform to the environmental regulations of the country of origin

Printed in China by Leo Paper Products, Heshan, Guangdong

1 3 5 7 9 10 8 6 4 2

The Naughty NAUGHTY Baddies

Mark Sperring

David Tazzyman

BLOOMSBURY

LONDON OXFORD NEW YORK NEW DELHI SYDNEY

Once there were FOUR
Naughty Naughty Baddies.

One

Two

Three   Four.

And each one was as **naughty** as the next.

The Naughty Naughty Baddies liked nothing more
than being WICKEDLY wicked,
AWFULLY awful and
DIABOLICALLY dreadful.

But best of all, the Naughty Naughty Baddies
loved to creep . . .

Creep

Creep

Creep

(They really were AWFULLY good at creeping!)

One **mischievous** day they were **creeping** about,
looking for something **naughty** to do . . .

They looked **this** way
and THAT,

THAT way
and **this**,

but they couldn't **spot** a single thing.

"Maybe we could STICK OUT our tongues and blow raspberries!" said **One**.

"Or JUMP in puddles and go home soaking wet!" said **Two**.

"Or PULL on a dangling thread and tie everyone up in naughty knots!" thought **Three**.

Miaow!

But **Four** had a plan – a plan so AWFULLY bad and WICKEDLY wicked that, if they were caught, something truly terrible would happen to them . . .

"We should JUMP on our trampoline . . ." said Four.

Boing

Boing

Boing!

"And BOUNCE into our Badmobile . . . ,"

"JUMP into a helicopter . . ."

Pht

pht

pht!

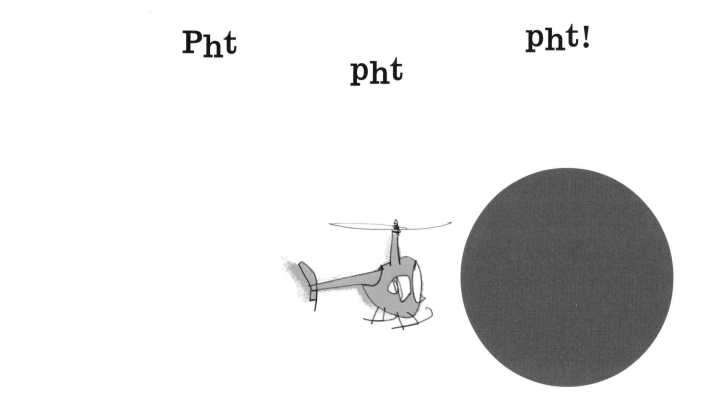

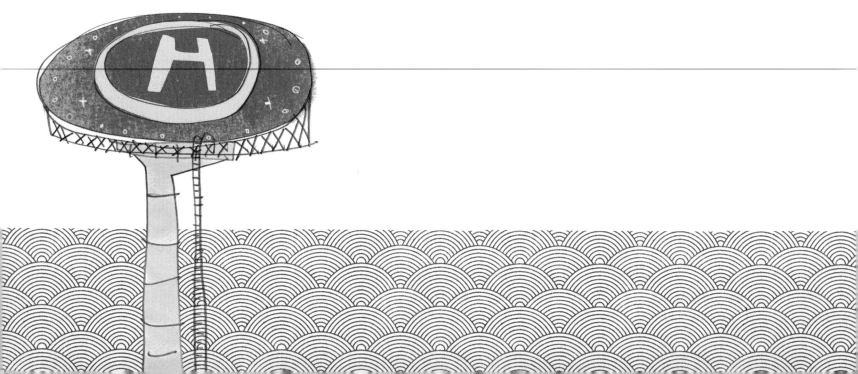

"PARACHUTE out over the royal palace . . ."

Wheeeeeee!

Arooooo!

"Then, and here's the wicked part . . ."

"STEAL all the **spots** off the
Queen's Little Doggy Woof-Woof!"

The Naughty Naughty Baddies grinned FIENDISH grins
and thought of all the DASTARDLY things they could
do with a swag bag full of STOLEN spots.

"We could make the WHOLE town go totally dotty!" they laughed. "And cause a right spot of bother. We could even creep into the zoo and create the world's FIRST . . ."

"Spot-adile!"

What a brilliantly bonkers, DARINGLY dastardly plan it was!

Mwa-ha-ha!

And in a matter of moments it was well and truly underway . . .

"Now for our **favourite** part,"
chuckled the Naughty Naughty Baddies.
"Time for a nice . . .
VILLAINOUS . . .
creep!"

Creep   **Creep**   **Creep**   They crept through the palace doors . . .

up
the
palace
stairs . . .

Creep

and past the palace guards . . .   **Creep**   **Creep**   **Creep**

Creep   **Creep**   and SNEAKILY past the King.

Then, holding their breath
and creeping more carefully
than ever, they crept quietly
into the throne room.

(Gosh, the Naughty Naughty Baddies
really were VERY good at creeping.)

As the Queen sat trying on crowns,
they SPOTTED their target,
snoozing happily in
its basket . . .

and without
further ado . . .

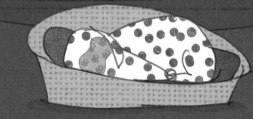

Creep

Creep

Creep

they carried out their
mischievous plan
to the dot!

What Naughty Naughty Baddies!

Everything had gone perfectly to plan,
but suddenly the sight of the Queen's spotless dog
struck them as WICKEDLY funny, and before they
could stop themselves . . .

they let out a
fiendish snigger.

Mwee-he-he!

The Naughty Naughty Baddies began to
Run Run Run but they weren't any good at running.
The Naughty Naughty Baddies were ONLY good at creeping.

And as they ran out of the room,

they tripped over

each other's feet . . .

"Ouch!"

bumped into the King . . .

"Sorry!"

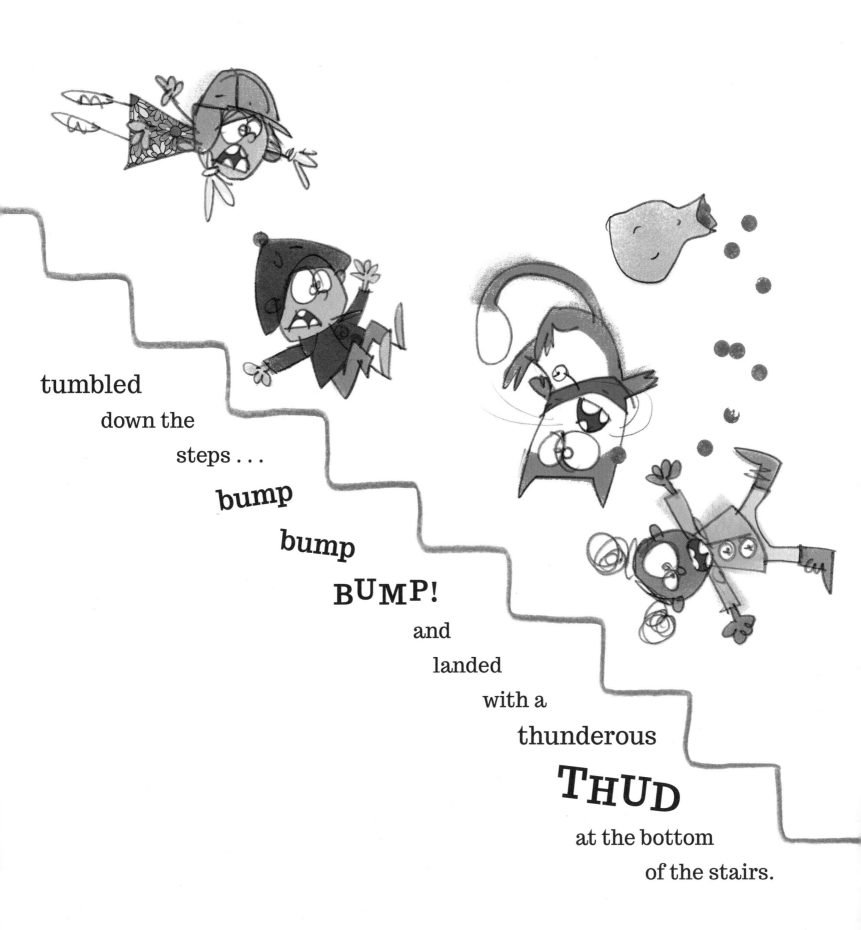

tumbled
down the
steps . . .
bump
bump
BUMP!
and
landed
with a
thunderous
THUD
at the bottom
of the stairs.

"It wasn't us!"
cried the Naughty Naughty Baddies.
But the evidence was clearly there for ALL to see
because, quite simply . . .

they were covered in
SPOTS!

"Throw them in JAIL!" shouted the guards.

"Send them to bed without any TEA!" bellowed the King.

"Let me chew and CHOMP on their heels!" snapped
the Little Doggy Woof-Woof (doing an excited little wee!).

"NO!" said the Queen,
because the Queen had a plan . . .

A plan so AWFULLY bad and WICKEDLY wicked
that everyone agreed it was the PERFECT punishment
for the Naughty Naughty Baddies . . .

"NO CREEPING
for a WHOLE week."

They could stand on TIPTOE and do twirly twirls
but NO creeping.

Twirl   Twirl   Twirly-TWIRL!

Oh dear, the Naughty Naughty Baddies HATE twirling.

BUT WHAT'S THIS?

A
dangling
thread . . .

Miaow!

It looks like the Naughty Naughty Baddies
have thought up yet another FIENDISH plan . . .

"Heeeeelp!"

Tying everyone up in WHIRLING

TWIRLING, naughty knots! Oh, MY!

What Naughty
Naughty Baddies!